By Jillian Powell

Illustrated by
Aleksandar Sotirovski

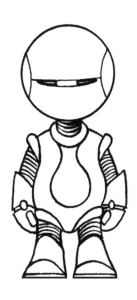

Titles in the Zipwire series:

Who Are You?	David Orme
3Dee	Danny Pearson
Doom Clone	Melanie Joyce
Too Risky!	Alison Hawes
Wanda Darkstar	Jane A C West
Galactic Games	Roger Hurn
Robot Eyes	Jillian Powell
Charlie's Tin	Lynda Gore
Run For Your Life	Jonny Zucker
Changing Rooms	Melanie Joyce

Badger Publishing Limited
Oldmedow Road, Hardwick Industrial Estate,
King's Lynn PE30 4JJ
Telephone: 01553 769209
www.badgerlearning.co.uk

2 4 6 8 10 9 7 5 3 1

Robot Eyes ISBN 978-1-78837-606-8

Badger Publishing would like to thank Jonny Zucker for his help
in putting this series together.

Commissioning Editor: Sarah Rudd
Editor: Claire Morgan
Typesetting: Adam Wilmott
Illustration: Aleksandar Sotirovski
Page 32 illustration: Juliet Breese
Cover design: Shaun Page
Font: OpenDyslexic

ROBOT EYES

Contents

Chapter 1

"Welcome to The Games, Tom and Ricky!" Mr Conor said. "You will be working in the athletes' village."

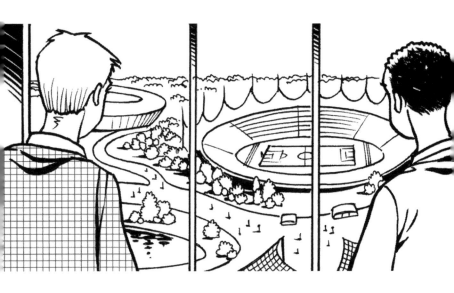

"This is an exciting year for us," added Mr Conor. "We are using robot helpers for the first time."

"Robots? Why do you need them?" asked Tom.

"These robots are super helpers. They can do all the tasks we need," replied Mr Conor.

As the boys left, a silver robot turned into Mr Conor's office.

Its red eyes fixed on Tom and Ricky and flashed.

Chapter 2

The next day, Tom and Ricky had a list of jobs to do.

They made their way to the athletes' village.

The little robot they had seen the day before was heading towards them.

Its red eyes flashed.

"Job done," it said in a flat robot voice.

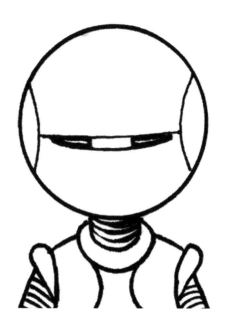

"What do you mean, job done?" asked Tom.

"Room keys. Welcome packs. Energy drinks. Job done," replied the robot.

"What? They were our jobs!"
Ricky said.

The robots eyes flashed red.

Then it turned and headed for
the Games Park.

Chapter 3

In the afternoon, Tom and Ricky had some free time.

Tom wanted to watch the pole vaulting.

The competition had just started.

"Look, the robot is there again," said Ricky. "What is it doing?"

"Be quiet! This guy is really good." replied Tom. "He has a world record."

The pole vaulter jumped.

He hit the bar and fell.

"That's really odd," said Tom, "He's the best."

A leaderboard was flashing beside the arena.

"There's one team winning all the events. I've never even heard of them!" said Ricky.

Tom shrugged.

"I can't get over that pole vaulter messing up," he said.

"It has happened to a few top athletes," Ricky pointed out.

On their way home, the boys
spotted a strange booth.

"Gobot..." Tom said, "I've seen
that somewhere..."

His mind flashed back to the
leaderboard.

"Gobot is a sponsor!" Tom cried.
"They sponsor the team that is
winning all the medals!"

Chapter 4

The next day, Tom borrowed his dad's camera.

"Something strange is going on," Tom said. "The camera might help us spot something. It's got lots of special functions."

The first event was the
long jump.

The robot was already there.

"The next guy to jump is favourite
to win. If I'm right, he will mess it
up," said Tom.

Tom aimed the camera.

The athlete jumped.

SPO

The crowd gasped.

It was a bad jump.

"Look!" Tom said to Ricky,
"I used the infra-red laser
detector."

Ricky stared at the image on
the camera.

"What is that?" he asked.

Ricky pointed to a ray of light
cutting across the image.

"THAT is why the top athletes have been messing up," said Tom. "Look where the light came from."

"The robot!" shouted Ricky. "Those red eyes!"

"The light blinds them for a second," Tom replied.

They looked over to where the robot had been.

It was gone.

The boys hurried to the next event. It was the 100 metres.

The robot was at the front of the crowd.

"Grab that flag," Tom told Ricky.

The boys crept behind the robot.

The starter gun went off.

At that exact moment, Tom waved the flag in front of the robot's eyes.

Its eyes flashed.

The crowd cheered.

The favourite runner had won.

Tom and Ricky looked for
the robot.

It was gone.

Chapter 5

Mr Conor stared at the image on the camera.

"This means we will have to run all the events again," he said.

"What about the robots?"
asked Ricky.

"We will shut down Gobot Inc."
Mr Conor replied.

As Tom and Ricky left the athletes' village, they saw a truck being loaded.

They were sure they saw some red eyes looking back at them.

Was it those red eyes that made their bikes crash into each other?

Questions

What colour is the robot? *(page 7)*

What jobs does the robot do instead of Ricky and Tom? *(page 10)*

What is the name on the side of the booth? *(page 17)*

What will happen to Gobot Inc.? *(page 26)*

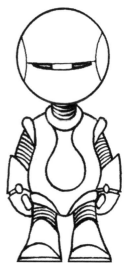

zipwire

Looking for your next read?

Have a look at all the great books in the Zipwire series

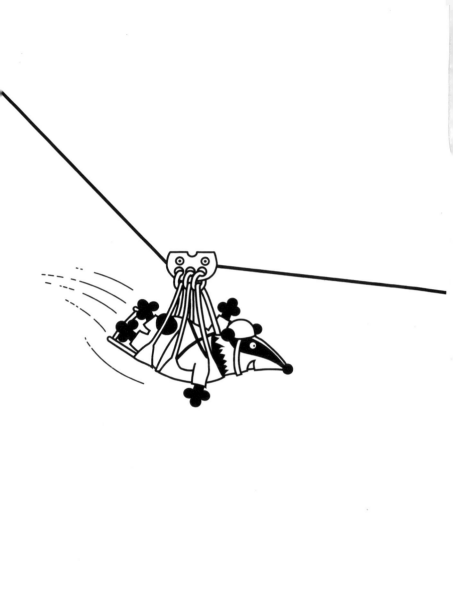